A Gift from Daniel

By Maria Le

Poses and layouts by Jason Fruchter

Ready-to-Read

Simon Spotlight

New York London Toronto Sydney New Delhi

SIMON SPOTLIGHT
An imprint of Simon & Schuster Children's Publishing Division
1230 Avenue of the Americas, New York, New York 10020
This Simon Spotlight edition August 2023
© 2023 The Fred Rogers Company
All rights reserved, including the right of reproduction in whole or in part in any form.
SIMON SPOTLIGHT, READY-TO-READ, and colophon are registered trademarks of
Simon & Schuster, Inc.
For information about special discounts for bulk purchases, please contact Simon & Schuster
Special Sales at 1-866-506-1949 or business@simonandschuster.com.
Manufactured in the United States of America 0723 LAK
2 4 6 8 10 9 7 5 3 1
ISBN 978-1-6659-4009-2 (hc)
ISBN 978-1-6659-4008-5 (pbk)
ISBN 978-1-6659-4010-8 (ebook)

Daniel Tiger and Miss Elaina are playing with dolls.

Daniel says to Miss Elaina, "I like playing with you."

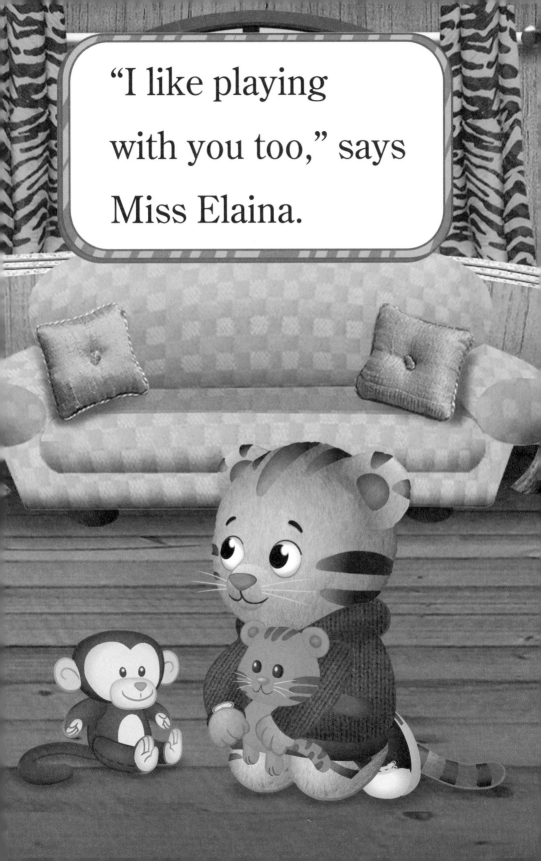

"I like playing with you too," says Miss Elaina.

"I have a gift for you," Miss Elaina says.

Miss Elaina gives
Daniel a toy robot.

Daniel is very happy. "Thank you! It is grr-ific!" he says.

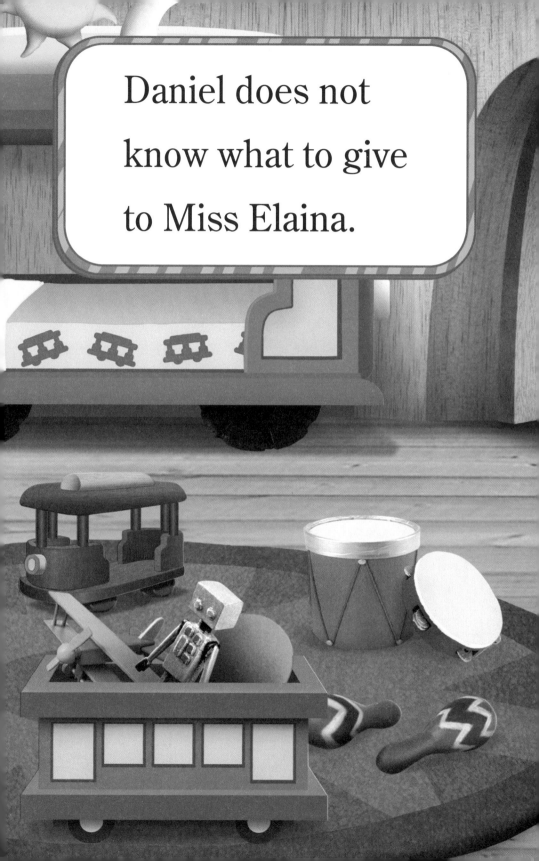

Mom Tiger says, "You can make a gift for Miss Elaina."

He uses paper and crayons to make a toy trolley for Miss Elaina.

Daniel visits Miss Elaina.
"I made a gift for you,"
Daniel says.

Daniel and Miss Elaina play with toy cars and the trolley.